D0493444

50000000084744

Hoping that all the Things in the world will get a little better

First published in 2019 by Child's Play (International) Ltd
Ashworth Road, Bridgemead, Swindon SN5 7YD, UK

Published in USA by Child's Play Inc
250 Minot Avenue, Auburn, Maine 04210

Distributed in Australia by Child's Play Australia Pty Ltd
Unit 10/20 Narabang Way, Belrose, Sydney, NSW 2085

Copyright © 2019 Petronela Dostalova
The moral rights of the author/illustrator have been asserted

All rights reserved

ISBN 978-1-78628-189-0
CLP170419CPLO6191890

Printed in Shenzhen, China

1 3 5 7 9 10 8 6 4 2

A catalogue record of this book
is available from the British Library

www.childs-play.com

The THINGS

PETRONELA DOSTALOVA

Meet Thing.

Thing's best friend is Cactus.
They play lots of games together.

Like pat-a-cake...

Ouch!

and tag.

Ouch!

and hopscotch...

Cactus is spiky, so sometimes
it hurts being friends.

Thing's other best friend is Moose the Shadow Puppet.
Moose only visits when the light is on.

Thing likes to play games with Moose, too...

...until it's time for bed.

Night, night,
Moose.

Come on, Cactus!
Bath time!

What do I look like, Cactus?
Am I red all over?
I wish I could see in
the broken mirror.

But Cactus can't see anything!

In the bath, Thing loves to talk to Cactus.

You are a good listener. You are very kind.

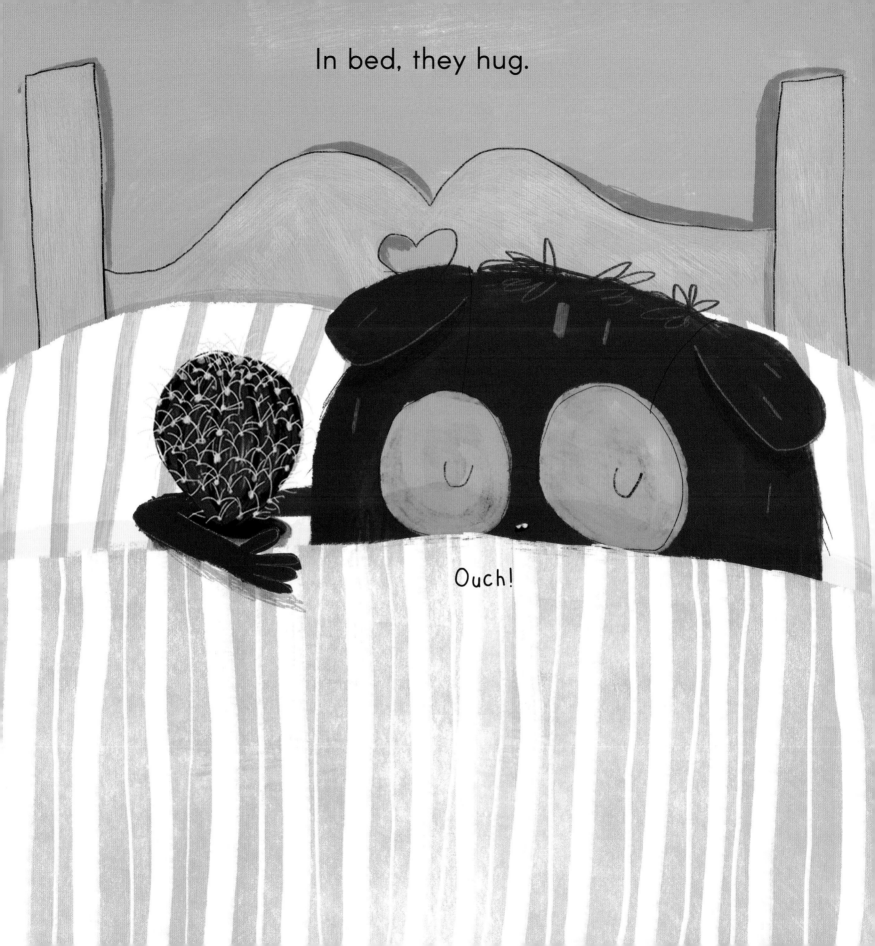

In bed, they hug.

Ouch!

One day, Thing was watching the world go by when it saw something strange.

Look, Cactus!

What is it?

It's an Other Thing!
It's going for a swim!

Other Thing was having a birthday party
with its friends, Mitten and Mitten.

Really?
You shouldn't have!

Other Thing made sandcastles on the beach...

...and played hide-and-seek
with Mitten and Mitten.

One hundred and three,
one hundred and four...

Thing was worried about Other Thing.

Other Thing
doesn't look like me.

Other Thing has big
floppy ears like these.

Other Thing wears silly clothes.
Just like these.

Though I do like its glasses.
They're a bit like mine.

Other Thing might not be friendly. It might take our things!

It is definitely a most dangerously dangerous Other Thing!

The next day, Thing was playing
with Cactus and Moose as usual...

when Moose
suddenly disappeared!

But they could not find
Moose anywhere at all.

I feel very sad.

Ouch!

Thing needed a big hug.
But it hurt.

Then all of a sudden Other Thing came along.

With the Mittens!

Hugging Cactus didn't hurt any more.
And being hugged was nice, too.

I haven't seen your
friend Moose.

Can we look for
him together?

The Things decided that they liked each other.

Thank you.

You're welcome.

And now they give each other presents all the time.

They tell each other how wonderful they are.

And they love to hug.

And guess who's back as well?

Thing will be pleased to see you!

And that's the way Things are.